Horror House
published in 2009 by
Hardie Grant Egmont
Ground Floor, Building 1, 658 Church Street
Richmond, Victoria 3121, Australia
www.hardiegrantegmont.com.au

A CiP record for this title is available from the National Library of Australia

Text copyright © 2009 H.I. Larry
Illustration and design copyright © 2009 Hardie Grant Egmont

Cover design by Andy Hook
Illustrations by Ron Monnier
Typeset by Ektavo

Printed in Australia by Griffin Press, an Accredited ISO AS/NZS
14001:2004 Environmental Management System printer.

7 9 10 8 6

The paper this book is printed on is certified against
the Forest Stewardship Council® Standards. Griffin Press
holds FSC chain of custody certification SGS-COC-005088.
FSC promotes environmentally responsible, socially beneficial
and economically viable management of the world's forests.

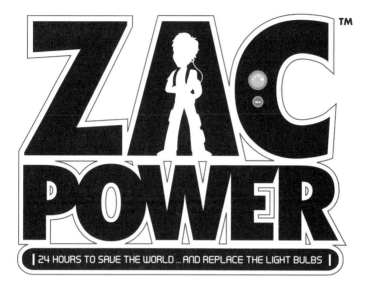

ZAC POWER™

24 HOURS TO SAVE THE WORLD ... AND REPLACE THE LIGHT BULBS

HORROR HOUSE
BY *H. I. LARRY*

ILLUSTRATIONS BY **RON MONNIER**

hardie grant EGMONT

CHAPTER... ...ONE

Zac Power rolled his eyes. His brother Leon was standing in the middle of the GIB hardware store, admiring a pair of standard-issue pliers.

'Look at these beauties!' exclaimed Leon.

Sometimes, Zac found it hard to believe that Leon was his brother. It was even harder to believe that Leon was a spy, working for a top-secret spy organisation called the Government Investigation Bureau, or GIB for short.

In fact, everyone in Zac's family was a spy – including Zac himself. He'd been around spies all his life. And he'd never seen one get excited about pliers before.

Still, Leon is more of a GIB inventor than a spy, Zac reminded himself. Leon was an expert in designing new spy gadgets. To him, a hardware store was better than a lolly shop. Especially an exclusive GIB hardware store like this one.

'OK, let's check out the energy-saving light bulbs,' said Leon, reluctantly putting the pliers down. 'Did you know that we can reduce our total annual carbon emissions by a huge amount once we've changed over all the light bulbs in our –'

'Yes, I know,' Zac interrupted. 'You've told me about a thousand times today, Leon.'

Zac glanced down at his watch.

Normally, Zac would have refused to spend his Saturday afternoon with Leon in a hardware store. But today he didn't have much choice. Tomorrow afternoon, Zac's school friends were going to see a movie called *Ghost Fighters*. Zac really wanted to go. He almost never did normal stuff with his friends because he was always going on GIB missions. But his parents had said that he could only go if he helped Leon with his latest geeky project – swapping all the light bulbs in their house for special energy-saving ones.

Trust Leon to be so boring, Zac groaned to himself. He pulled out his SpyPad, the hand-held mini-computer that all GIB spies used. Wasn't there an important mission or something that GIB could send him on?

When Zac went to check his messages,

though, there was no signal. He gave his SpyPad a shake, but nothing happened.

Zac frowned at the screen. 'I don't think my SpyPad's connected to Headquarters,' he told Leon.

'Maybe your battery is flat,' suggested Leon, studying a very large screwdriver. 'That sometimes kills the signal. There's a recharge station in the store. One of the auto-drive electric buggies will take you straight there.'

Zac shrugged. He didn't think the battery was flat as he'd only charged it yesterday. But it was a good excuse to get away from Leon and his energy-saving light bulbs!

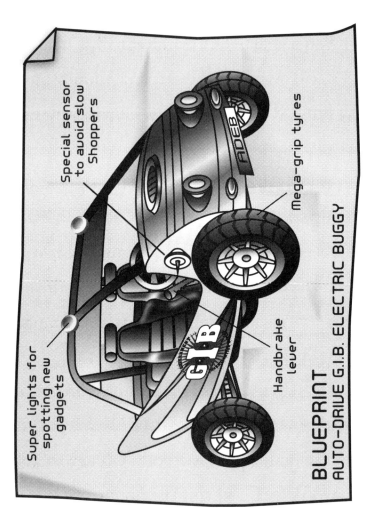

Super lights for
spotting new
gadgets

Special sensor
to avoid slow
Shoppers

Mega-grip tyres

Handbrake
lever

BLUEPRINT
AUTO-DRIVE G.I.B. ELECTRIC BUGGY

'Back soon, Leon!' he said, throwing his backpack into the front seat of a nearby GIB buggy. He hopped in and selected Recharge Station on the destination panel as the buggy zoomed off.

'Recharge Station selected,' an electronic voice said. It looked like the buggy was set to Chat Mode. 'Due to unknown causes, the whole city is experiencing power surges. Please note that your SpyPad might be affected.'

ZZZZZT!

Suddenly, there was a loud buzzing noise and the entire store was plunged into total darkness. Even worse, the buggy had gone out of control!

BRRRM!

It raced around the pitch-black hardware store, screeching around corners and bouncing off shelves. Zac wrestled with the controls, trying to find the manual steering wheel. He had no idea why a black-out would make the buggy go crazy. And he had to figure out how to get it to stop!

SCREEEK!

The buggy screeched wildly and pushed through what felt like heavy plastic doors.

There's got to be a handbrake somewhere on this thing, Zac thought. Holding tightly to his seat with one hand, he felt beneath the seat with the other.

When he found the brake, he gripped

it hard and wrenched it upwards. The buggy immediately braked, but instead of stopping, it started spinning wildly.

Oh, no, Zac groaned to himself, trying not to fall out of his seat. *Braking with a handbrake always causes burn-outs!*

He held onto his seat as hard as he could, but he could feel his fingers slipping. He tensed up, preparing to go flying out of the spinning buggy.

Just as he was about to lose his grip completely, the store lights crackled back to life. The buggy did one last donut on the concrete floor and then pulled smoothly to a stop. Zac could smell burning rubber in the air.

He carefully climbed out of the buggy and looked around. It seemed that he was in a storage area out the back of the hardware store.

I wonder if my SpyPad's working yet? Zac thought, reaching into his pocket and taking it out.

The SpyPad screen flickered to life. He still didn't have a signal. But there was something very strange on the screen. *Very* strange indeed.

Zac had received a mission on his SpyPad. But it wasn't from GIB!

CHAPTER ... TWO

Zac knew that GIB usually sent out their missions on special coded disks. It was very risky to send a mission directly to SpyPads because it could be hacked into.

But Zac also knew that other spy agencies weren't so careful. He quickly scanned the message on his SpyPad.

CLASSIFIED BIG MISSION

MISSION INITIATED: 10.00AM
CURRENT TIME: 2.30PM

BIG data indicates that there is an
unusually high level of storm activity
at the mansion at 13 Grande Street.
Your mission is to investigate
the gathering storm clouds.

We suspect that GIB has come up
with a gadget to control the weather!
The BIG radar predicts that a major
storm will break at 10.00am tomorrow.
You MUST be at the top of the mansion when
the storm hits to witness what happens.

Go to the mansion immediately to
monitor any suspicious activity.

NB: The mansion is said to be haunted.

HORROR HOUSE
>>> ON

Zac's mouth dropped open. *This message was meant for a BIG agent!* But how did it get on his SpyPad? And why did BIG think that GIB were controlling the weather? It didn't seem like a very GIB thing to do.

I guess the power surges must have made my SpyPad pick up a transmission, he thought.

But his SpyPad still didn't have a signal, and Zac's spy senses were tingling. Something wasn't right.

He decided to go straight to 13 Grande Street and check it out. When his SpyPad had a stronger signal, he would call HQ for back-up.

Zac wondered briefly if he should tell Leon where he was going. *No,* he thought, rolling his eyes. *Leon is happy looking at light bulbs. I'll call him later.*

First of all, Zac had to figure out how to get to 13 Grande Street. *I suppose I could take that crazy GIB hardware store buggy, but...*

Then he had a brainwave. He could take a GIB Commuter-Scooter! These were small, zippy scooters that GIB parked at various handy points around the city. They were for emergency spy travel.

Zac looked around. There was bound to be a Commuter-Scooter near the GIB hardware store. Sure enough, parked across the street was a shiny green scooter with the word *Dragonfly* painted on the side. It wasn't exactly the sort of super-fast, high-tech vehicle that Zac was used to driving. But it would do.

Zac hopped on and swiped the scooter's controls with his GIB ID card.

BRO_{OOO}MMM_M!

Not bad! Zac grinned. The machine actually had some grunt! He flicked the scooter into gear and took off.

He sped down the city streets, weaving in and out of traffic. He was pretty sure he knew the way to 13 Grande Street, but he decided to punch in the coordinates to the Dragonfly's GPS anyway.

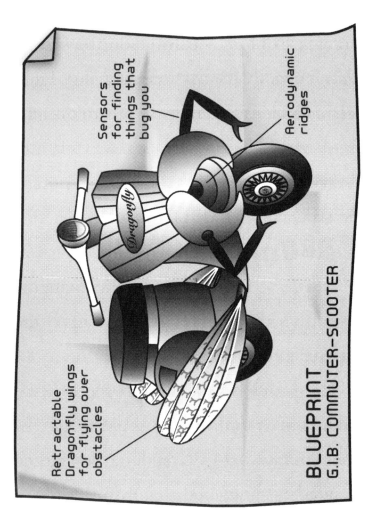

Sensors for finding things that bug you

Aerodynamic ridges

Retractable Dragonfly wings for flying over obstacles

Dragonfly

BLUEPRINT
G.I.B. COMMUTER-SCOOTER

After a bit of expert driving, Zac noticed that the Dragonfly's left handlebar was suddenly glowing bright green. *I guess that means I should turn left,* Zac thought, pressing hard on the accelerator. The Dragonfly skimmed the road lightly and barely tilted as Zac took the corner at full speed.

The scooter kept telling him when to turn left and right, and pretty soon Zac arrived at the mansion.

Zac parked the Dragonfly on the kerb, looking around as he climbed off. The other houses in the street looked perfectly normal. But the house at 13 Grande Street was *totally* different.

For one thing, it was a huge mansion. It also looked really old and dirty. Zac couldn't imagine anyone ever living there.

'Creepy, isn't it?' said a voice behind him.

Zac jumped. But it was just a sweet old lady, smiling at him. She reminded Zac of his granny, especially because she smelt so strongly of lavender. The only thing slightly weird about her was that she had lots of purple hair. It looked like a wig!

Thinking quickly, Zac pretended to look upset. 'My football went over the fence,' he said. 'I have to get it.'

'You can't go in there, sonny!' exclaimed the old lady, looking horrified. 'It's haunted! Stay well away.'

Then she patted him on the arm and hurried off.

Zac waited until she was out of sight. Then he slipped through the front gate, smirking. Haunted – as if!

That was where this old lady and his granny were different. Zac's granny was a top GIB spy. She would never believe some stupid haunted house story.

THERE'S NO SUCH THING AS GHOSTS.
– Zac's granny (Agent Wrinkles) –

G·I·B

The same went for Zac. And the more he was told to stay out of somewhere, the more determined he was to go in.

I just don't know why BIG want their agent to wait around at this mansion until tomorrow morning, Zac thought, shaking his head. *What am I supposed to do until then?*

CHAPTER... THREE

Even Zac had to admit that the yard of 13 Grande Street was pretty creepy. Everything was completely still.

Zac touched one of the plants and realised why. It was completely hard! Almost like it was made out of stone. And if that wasn't creepy enough, the yard also had a cemetery in it.

The house itself wasn't any nicer. The paint was peeling and the eaves were covered with cobwebs. Right at the top of the house was a tower with a spooky-looking window.

That must be the room that BIG meant, realised Zac, glancing down at his watch.

It was only late afternoon, but already the garden seemed very dark. Thick storm clouds were blocking out the sun. And they seemed particularly thick around the tower at the top of the mansion.

There was a sudden crash of lightning and rain started drizzling down. Zac raced for the porch.

As he ran, Zac saw two things that would've been enough to make any normal kid turn and run straight home. First, all the lights in the house flashed on. And then, Zac saw the outline of a figure standing at the top window!

Then the lights flickered off and the figure disappeared.

Zac reached the steps leading up to the porch. His heart was pounding. *Not because I'm scared, though,* he told himself. *It's just because I had to run.* He took a deep breath and started walking quietly up the stairs towards the front door.

Lucky I wore my new sound-absorbing Sneaky Sneakers today, he thought.

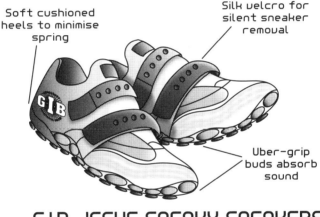

Soft cushioned heels to minimise spring

Silk velcro for silent sneaker removal

Uber-grip buds absorb sound

G.I.B.—ISSUE SNEAKY SNEAKERS

He knew he had to be extra careful on this mission. His SpyPad still didn't have any signal to HQ, and GIB had no idea where he was. Plus it was really important that

BIG didn't know he was here, either. He was crashing a top-secret BIG mission!

So I guess I'm hiding here for the next 17 hours! Zac groaned to himself.

He put his head against the front door and listened. He thought he could hear something moving inside. It was a sort of rustling sound. Was it the figure he'd seen in the tower? Or was it a BIG agent who'd received the same mission Zac's SpyPad had?

Suddenly, something hairy brushed against Zac's neck. He spun around. There was an enormous spider web! And right in the middle of the web was a massive spider with two nasty-looking fangs.

Zac shrugged. It was just a huntsman spider, and he wasn't scared of them. Sure, it was huge, but Zac knew it wouldn't bite him.

'Sorry, little fella,' grinned Zac, stepping around the web.

Then Zac remembered something about huntsman spiders that he'd seen on Leon's favourite TV show, *Creepy Creatures.*

Huntsman spiders never spin webs. They catch their prey by chasing them.

CREEPY CREATURES

This spider has a web, thought Zac, *so it must be a fake!* He reached carefully into the web and grabbed the spider. Sure enough, it was made of latex.

It's very realistic, thought Zac, impressed. *Whoever made it must have REALLY wanted to scare people away.* He dropped it into his backpack. It would come in handy the next time he wanted to play a joke on Leon.

Then Zac grabbed hold of the door handle. Time to start investigating. But the moment he began turning the handle, Zac heard a loud, spooky voice.

KEEEEP OoooOOuuuUT!

What IS that? thought Zac. He took his hand off the door handle and the voice stopped.

Someone is up to something here, thought Zac, checking the door. Sure enough, he saw a wire running from the handle of the door, up along the door-frame and disappearing into the walls.

Zac shook his head and pushed open the door. The voice spoke again.

ABANDON ALL HOPE, YE WHO ENTER!

Yeah, whatever! Zac thought, stepping inside. He wasn't scared, but he was on full alert. Whoever was in here would definitely know that Zac was inside the mansion, after all the noise that door had made.

CHAPTER FOUR

Inside the mansion it was pitch black. But Zac could clearly make out that strange rustling sound he'd heard through the door before. Now he could hear squeaking, too. As Zac's eyes adjusted to the blackness, he saw dark, winged shapes hanging from the roof.

Oh, gross, thought Zac. *I hate bats!*

He tip-toed quietly across the room, trying not to disturb them. But then he tripped over on the edge of a carpet.

CRASH!

Suddenly, the squeaking got incredibly loud. A moment later, Zac was mobbed by hundreds of cold, furious bats, flapping their wings in his face and screeching so loudly that he thought his eardrums would burst.

Zac tried to push his way through the angry bats. But then they swarmed together and linked up all their claws. Zac found himself facing one enormous super-bat!

There's no way I'm fighting that thing!

thought Zac. There had to be a way to escape!

Then Zac remembered something Leon had said about a new feature on the SpyPad called the Sonic Scrambler.

'Bats have super-sensitive hearing,' Leon had explained. 'And they rely on sound to navigate. If you turn on the Sonic Scrambler, they'll go nuts!'

With one hand shielding his face from the super-bat's sharp claws, Zac quickly selected the Sonic Scrambler on his Spypad and pushed the button.

Nothing happened. Nothing that Zac could hear, anyway. It was a different story for the bats. They instantly stopped squeaking and dropped out of the super-bat formation.

Then the bats started doing somersaults in the air at top speed, and crashing through a window to get outside. They moved so fast that they were nothing but a big, batty blur.

No real bat could move that fast, thought Zac, suspicious. He reached out and grabbed one.

It felt cold and hard – not like a living creature at all. Sure enough, when Zac flipped the bat over, he saw 'AcroBat' stamped on the back. It was just a robot. He let go of it and the AcroBat immediately whizzed out the window with the others.

ACROBAT™

Right, thought Zac, checking the time on his watch. *What should I do now?*

He decided to kill time by playing a few games on his SpyPad.

There's plenty of time to check out the mansion later, he figured, picking a dark corner and sitting down against the wall.

Zac yawned and opened his eyes. For a moment, he had no idea where he was. Then he remembered that he was crashing a BIG mission in a supposedly haunted mansion.

Must have fallen asleep, he thought, stretching. He stood up and checked the time on his watch.

As Zac's eyes adjusted to the dark, he saw a dusty wooden staircase leading upstairs.

I guess I'd better do some investigating, he thought. *I bet that staircase leads to the tower.*

Zac started climbing the stairs. He had to push his way through giant spider webs, which were thick and stickier than super glue. He had only just reached the first floor when he heard something that made him freeze.

THUMP-THUMP-THUMP!

The noise was coming from the cupboard on the landing. Someone – or something – was in there, banging loudly. Zac took one cautious step towards the cupboard.

THWHACK! THWHACK!

The banging was getting louder. Then another sound joined in.

WHOoOOooo!

Zac gulped. *There's NO SUCH THING as ghosts,* he reminded himself. *I'll just open the cupboard and everything will be explained. It's not like a ghost is going to come floating out.* Zac reached over and flung the cupboard door open.

WHOoOOooo!

Instantly, a white shape rushed out of the cupboard. And it headed straight for Zac!

CHAPTER FIVE

Quickly, Zac grabbed hold of the white shape and yanked hard. It was just a sheet, and underneath was someone with a very familiar face.

'Caz?' Zac gasped.

Caz Rewop was the last person Zac ever wanted to run into on a mission. She was the sneakiest, meanest BIG agent Zac had ever met. *But hang on,* thought Zac, confused. *If this is Caz, why is she suddenly really tall?*

'I'm not Caz,' said the girl, looking frightened. 'I'm her big sister. Who are you? What are you doing here?'

'Er, I'm here because I was sent a BIG mission,' said Zac.

'Oh, so you work for BIG, too!' said the girl, looking relieved. 'I'm so glad you're here. I've just joined BIG and this is my first solo mission. Everyone thinks that I'm going to be just as brilliant as Caz. But I'm not. I'm good at inventing gadgets, but I'm hopeless at dealing with haunted houses. It's way too scary!'

Then she smiled and stuck out her hand for Zac to shake. 'I'm Agent Gadget Girl,' she said, 'but just call me Leonie.'

She has no idea who I am, thought Zac. *Perfect!* Leonie could be a useful source of information for this mission.

'I'm, er, Agent Choir Boy,' said Zac, thinking fast. Zac's *real* code name was Agent Rock Star.

'Maybe we can work together?' suggested Leonie hopefully. 'I've got heaps of my own cool gadgets we can use. And the mansion's floor plans are on my SpyDevice – want to see?'

She stuck out her SpyDevice for Zac to have a look.

'Sure, let's work together. I was scared, too,' lied Zac as he checked out the floor plans. It seemed like SpyDevices were the BIG version of a SpyPad.

'Cool bananas!' grinned Leonie.

Zac choked back a laugh. He couldn't help liking Leonie, even though she was a BIG agent *and* Caz's sister. The only other person who would say something as tragic as 'cool bananas' was his own geeky brother.

'Let's go, then,' said Zac. 'I still haven't been up to the room at the top of the tower.'

But just then, they heard another sound.

HA HA HAAARAH!

Leonie grabbed Zac's arm very tightly.

'I heard that spooky laughter before,' she whimpered. 'That's why I hid in the cupboard with a sheet over my head.

I thought if a monster found me, they would think I was a ghost and leave me alone.'

'I think it's just someone trying to scare us,' said Zac.

'Well, it's working,' wailed Leonie. 'Let's leave!'

'No,' said Zac firmly. 'Let's go exploring.'

The sound was coming from behind a nearby door. Zac strode over.

'Don't open it!' pleaded Leonie.

I'll show her that there's nothing to be afraid of, decided Zac, pushing open the door.

It sounded like a dinner party was going on in there. Zac could hear glasses clinking and cutlery scraping across plates. There was also lots of laughing and talking. But it was too dark to see anything.

'Do you have a torch on you?' Zac whispered to Leonie.

'No, but I've got a Lightning Ball,' Leonie whispered back. She handed him something small and round, about the size a bubble-gum ball. 'When it bounces, it makes a flash of light that lasts for about thirty seconds. But I think we should just leave now, while we still –'

'No, let's see what's going on,' replied Zac. Then he threw the Lightning Ball into the room. There was a bang, and instantly, the room was lit up like someone had set off a flare.

In the middle of the room was a big table laid out for a dinner party with fine china and crystal glasses. And seated around the table were eight guests. Eight skeleton guests! They were cutting invisible food with their knives and lifting empty glasses up to their mouths as if they were drinking.

'Aaaaah!' shrieked Leonie.

CHAPTER ... SIX

Instantly, all the skeletons started waving their bony arms towards Zac and Leonie, laughing nastily.

'Calm down, Leonie,' Zac hissed. 'It obviously can't be real. Have you got another light source?'

'Can't we just go?' whimpered Leonie.

'No,' said Zac firmly. 'We're staying.'

'Well, that was my last Lightning Ball,' sighed Leonie, 'but I've got a Fandle.'

'What's a Fandle?' asked Zac.

Leonie handed Zac what looked like a stick with a tiny, glowing light bulb on the top. On the side was a small rotor. A breeze blowing through the broken window was making it turn.

'The spinning fan powers the light,' explained Leonie.

'Nice!' said Zac, impressed. He held the Fandle out and took a few steps towards the dinner party. The skeletons were still stretching out their arms and chortling. But Zac wasn't worried.

He examined the skeletons carefully.

'Just as I thought,' he told Leonie. 'They're puppets.'

SKELE-FAKE™

Zac showed Leonie the wire attached to the skeletons' bones. 'See? These wires are connected to pulleys hidden up in the ceiling. There's a machine up there that's making them rise and fall so it looks like the skeletons are moving by themselves.'

'But what about the laughing and talking?' whispered Leonie, still scared.

Zac shone the Fandle over one of the bowls on the table. Hidden inside was a tiny MP3 player.

'There you go,' he said. 'There's always a logical explanation.'

Oh, no, Zac thought to himself. He was beginning to sound like Leon!

'Um, Agent Choir Boy?' said Leonie,

raising an eyebrow. 'What's the logical explanation for that?'

Zac turned and found himself staring right into the glowing red eyes of a large, purple floating blob. Actually, he was staring *through* it, as the blob was totally transparent. Zac gulped. This thing looked exactly like a ghost. But that wasn't possible, was it?

'Run!' shouted Leonie.

'It's probably just a hologram,' said Zac, more confidently than he felt. If it really was a hologram, it looked very realistic.

'It's not a hologram,' said Leonie. 'Holograms can't move through three dimensional space like *that*!'

Zac glanced over his shoulder. Sure enough, the ghost had started gliding towards them!

Leonie took off down the dark corridor, and Zac followed. He wasn't scared, because he was pretty sure this thing was another trick. But he couldn't risk losing sight of Leonie. She had the gadgets, after all. And the map!

'Dead end!' called Leonie, stopping suddenly. 'We're doomed!'

Up ahead, the corridor was completely blocked by a floor-to-ceiling bookcase.

Zac stopped and looked around. The ghost hovered in front of them. Then Zac noticed something weird. The ghost was flickering, like it was being turned on and off.

Hang on, thought Zac, shining the Fandle around the corridor.

'Leonie, look!' he said, pointing.

There were rows of tiny lights in the floor. And there were heaps more in the ceiling and along the walls.

Leonie looked carefully at the lights. 'Wow,' she said, suddenly completely unafraid. 'This ghost is a volumetric display! You know, a hologram projected from six different directions.'

'Are you sure?' asked Zac. He could remember Leon once telling him something about this. 'I thought volumetric displays were only in the early stages of development.'

'Yeah, this is cutting edge stuff,' said Leonie. 'So, what do we do now? I think we're stuck.'

Zac had to agree that things looked bad. On one side of them was the bookcase. On the other was the volumetric display ghost. There was no way Zac was pushing through that thing. The way it was buzzing and sparking told him that it was electrified.

He checked his watch.

There were still four hours until the storm was due to strike and he had to be up in the tower.

What are we supposed to do until then? thought Zac, leaning heavily against the bookcase. *Just wait around until the ghost leaves us alone?*

The bookcase begin to shift, and before Zac could move, it had spun around like a revolving door. Then the ground gave way beneath his feet, and Zac fell heavily into the darkness.

CHAPTER... SEVEN

Zac blinked in the darkness and sat up woozily. His head felt sore. He must have bumped it on the way down. He guessed he'd been passed out for an hour or two.

'Stupid revolving bookshelf!' he muttered to himself. 'I should have seen that coming.'

Zac looked around. The room was very

dark because there weren't any windows. The only light was coming from a vent near the ceiling. *I'm in the cellar,* he realised.

Nearby was a stack of boxes. Instantly, Zac's spy senses started tingling. The boxes looked brand new – not like things that had been stored in a cellar for years and years. Zac inspected one of the box labels.

Zac got up and opened the box. It was filled with a greyish, chalky powder. It looked exactly like real dust, but for some reason it smelt like flowers.

The next box Zac opened was filled with small, squeezy bottles labelled INSTANT SPIDER WEBS. When Zac opened a bottle and squeezed it, strings of clear glue shot out and attached themselves to the wall. They looked like the webs he'd fought through while climbing the stairs.

Hmmm, fake dust and fake spider webs, thought Zac. *Looks like someone's been trying really hard to make this place seem like an old haunted house.*

Nearby he could hear a low, humming noise. Zac tracked the sound to a large metal machine. Every now and then a little puff of steam came out of it and then disappeared through the ceiling vent.

It's some kind of generator, realised Zac. *But what is it for?*

Then he saw a little label on the side of the machine. He crouched down to read it. It said: *StormGenerator BIG-prototype DC76/14.* Zac's skin crawled. BIG were making the storms! So why would they send their *own* agent to investigate?

Just then, a trapdoor in the ceiling burst open and a figure dropped through.

'Agent Choir Boy?' whispered a familiar voice. 'Are you in here?'

'Over here, Leonie,' Zac called out.

Leonie rushed over. 'I've been searching for you everywhere!' she exclaimed. 'One minute you were standing right beside me and then suddenly you'd disappeared. It's taken me ages to find you.'

Then there was a rumble of thunder and a crash of lightning.

'There's a big storm coming,' Leonie said nervously. 'We should probably stay down here till it passes.'

Zac glanced at his watch. He had to be in the room at the top of the tower when the storm hit!

'Leonie, we have to get up to the tower room,' said Zac urgently. 'Remember the mission? We're supposed to be up there when the storm breaks. And it sounds like the storm's coming now!'

'I'm not going anywhere,' Leonie whispered, terrified.

Zac sighed. *If only Leonie were a bit braver,* he thought. Then he remembered something. At Agent Hammer's birthday party last week, Zac had got a packet of fake No-Fear Gum in the lollybag.

Of course there was no such thing as *real* No-Fear Gum, but the idea was that whoever chewed the gum instantly looked tougher. And if they looked tougher, they felt tougher.

It's just what Leonie needs, thought Zac.

He looked through his backpack to find the lollybag.

'Hey, Leonie,' said Zac, taking out the gum and offering her a piece. 'Do you want some No-Fear Gum? It's special, er, BIG-issue. It's supposed to stop you feeling scared.'

Leonie looked doubtful, but took a piece anyway.

'Hey, I think it's working,' she said as she started chewing. 'Maybe we should go up to the tower after all.' She jumped to her feet. 'Come on, I'll use my DOLL to find out if there's a secret passage in here.'

'Your *doll?*' said Zac. 'Aren't you a bit old for dolls?'

'DOLL is short for Door Or Lock Locator,' explained Leonie, opening her bag and taking out what looked like a particularly creepy doll. 'If it's pointed at a secret passage or concealed entrance, the eyes light up. Watch.'

Leonie swung the DOLL around the room. Sure enough, after a few moments, the eyes started flashing.

Zac shuddered. 'That's the scariest thing I've seen all day,' he said under his breath.

Leonie raced over to one of the walls and gave it a whack with the DOLL. Instantly, a panel slid back, revealing a narrow

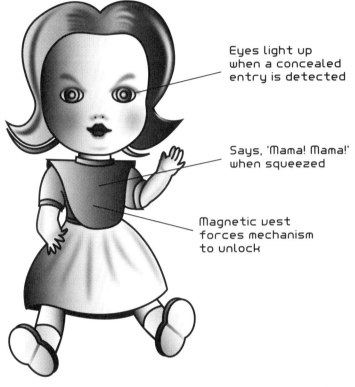

Eyes light up
when a concealed
entry is detected

Says, 'Mama! Mama!'
when squeezed

Magnetic vest
forces mechanism
to unlock

D.O.L.L. – Door Or Lock Locator

entranceway with steps leading up.

Leonie pulled out her SpyDevice and
checked the map. 'These steps lead right

up to the tower room,' she said, putting her SpyDevice away. 'Are you ready, Agent Choir Boy?'

'Let's do it,' said Zac firmly.

CHAPTER... EIGHT

Leonie bounced up the stairs, still chewing on the fake No-Fear Gum. 'Hurry up!' she barked over her shoulder.

Zac rolled his eyes. The new, super-brave Leonie was also super-bossy!

Then Zac spotted something that froze him to the spot. Up ahead was a figure, lurking in the shadows.

'Wait, Leonie,' he warned. 'It could be an ambush.'

But Leonie laughed and kept going. 'It's just an old suit of armour!' she said, shining the Fandle on the figure.

But Zac's spy senses were still on full alert. 'Don't touch it,' he told her.

'I can't believe that this time *you're* scared and *I'm* not!' giggled Leonie, knocking on the suit with her knuckles.

SWAT!

Then the Knight raised one arm and pushed Leonie over!

'Aaah!' squealed Leonie, tumbling backwards. Zac leapt forwards and caught her.

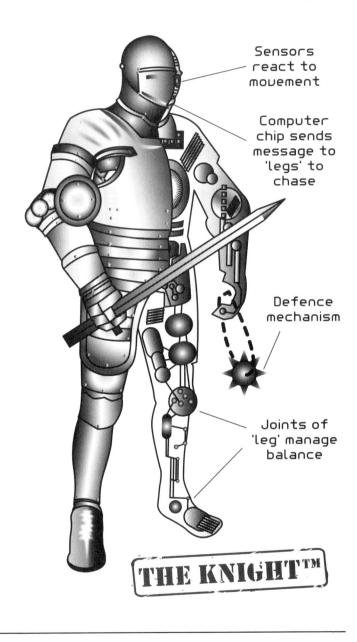

Sensors react to movement

Computer chip sends message to 'legs' to chase

Defence mechanism

Joints of 'leg' manage balance

THE KNIGHT™

In one hand, the Knight held a gleaming sword. In the other was a spiky ball and chain, which it was whizzing around over its head! The Knight took a threatening step towards them.

'Got anything that might help us out here, Leonie?' muttered Zac.

'Just this,' said Leonie, pulling out her hairclip. 'It's a super-strong magnet. Maybe we could stick the Knight's legs together?'

'Great!' said Zac, impressed.

'On the count of three,' said Leonie. 'One, two ... *three!*'

Zac ran up and grabbed the Knight's legs, while Leonie slipped the magnet onto one of its knees. The magnet instantly stuck the Knight's legs together.

'Run!' yelled Leonie, heading up the stairs.

Zac wasn't far behind. But a moment later...

CLUNK!

Leonie and Zac leapt up the stairs two at a time. But the Knight was dragging itself up the stairs behind them.

CLANK! CLUNK! CLANK!

There was a door at the top of the stairs. *That must be the door to the tower room,* thought Zac. He rattled the handle, but it was locked.

'What do we do now?' asked Leonie.

Thinking quickly, Zac fished around in his pocket and pulled out his keys.

Door key, bike key, locker key, thought Zac, flipping through them. Finally, he found what he was looking for – a skeleton key. It was meant to open almost any door in the world. Leon had given it to him ages ago, but Zac had never tried it out before.

'Hurry!' warned Leonie. 'The Knight's coming closer!'

Zac could still hear the clanking sound of the Knight dragging itself up the stairs. He stuck the skeleton key into the lock. It turned, but then got stuck and refused to budge.

The clanking sound grew louder and

louder. Then suddenly Leonie leapt down a few steps towards the Knight and karate-kicked it away.

'Heee-YA!' she yelled.

The Knight fell back down the stairs with a huge crash.

'I didn't know you knew karate!' said Zac, raising an eyebrow.

'I don't,' grinned Leonie.

Zac shook his head and laughed. Maybe that No-Fear Gum was real, after all!

He forced the skeleton key to twist in the lock, and finally the door opened. Zac and Leonie flung themselves into the room and banged the door shut behind them.

The room was dark and smelt strongly

of flowers. In fact, it smelt like lavender.

Just like that fake dust, realised Zac. *And that little old lady who told me not to come in here!*

Leonie nudged him. 'Um, Agent Choir Boy?' she muttered. 'We're not alone.'

She pointed to a big chair in the middle of the room. It was rocking backwards and forwards. Slowly, the chair swung around.

CHAPTER... NINE

'Welcome, agents,' said the person in the chair. 'Congratulations on passing the test.'

It was the sweet old lady he'd met the day before. But her weird purple hair was gone, and she was wearing a BIG uniform! Zac shot a look at Leonie. Did she know who this BIG person was?

Leonie was standing to attention. 'Agent

Gadget Girl at your service, Commander Big Wig!' she said excitedly. 'What's the test?'

'This whole mansion is one big test,' replied Commander Big Wig smoothly. 'It was created to trial BIG's top-secret new scaring technology.'

Zac's mind was ticking over. Of course his SpyPad hadn't intercepted that BIG mission – it hadn't even *had* a signal! BIG must have scrambled his reception and then planted the message.

'You wanted us to come here as guinea pigs,' said Zac, shaking his head.

'Exactly, Agent Rock Star,' smiled Big Wig. 'But you and Gadget Girl are the first agents to actually make it to the top.'

'Hang on,' frowned Leonie. 'This is Agent Choir Boy, not Agent Rock Star.'

'Wrong,' said Big Wig. 'Obviously, the ultimate test of our scaring technology would be if it worked on GIB agents. That's why we sent the mission to Agent Rock Star, the most fearless spy in the business.'

Leonie stared at Zac. 'You're a GIB agent?'

'Well, yes,' Zac admitted.

'You lied to me!' yelled Leonie.

'Enough bickering,' growled the Commander. 'I haven't finished telling you about this place!'

Zac's mind was going a million miles

an hour. Why was Big Wig so keen to tell them about the mansion if it was secret technology? And how was he going to get out of there?

'The whole place is powered by storm energy,' explained the Commander proudly. 'That storm generator in the cellar creates the storm clouds over the mansion, which then makes thunder and lightning. The lightning zaps a power-grid on the roof and sends electricity surging through the entire building.'

Then Zac realised something. 'Is that why all the city's appliances have been on the blink recently?' he asked. 'Because you're generating so much electricity here?'

'Correct,' grinned Big Wig nastily. 'And we've been able to use it to manipulate your private mobile networks, Rock Star. Tell me, does your SpyPad have a signal yet?'

Zac said nothing. He knew it didn't.

Commander Big Wig turned to Leonie. 'Agent Gadget Girl, as you've passed the test, you will now be made a BIG field agent.'

Leonie looked proud. *She won't be a fearless field agent once she stops chewing that fake No-Fear Gum,* thought Zac, annoyed.

'What about you, Rock Star?' smirked Big Wig. 'I can make you an official BIG field agent too, if you want.'

'No way!' snapped Zac. 'Firstly, I'm not a girl like your other agents. And secondly, I'm not evil.'

'Your stupidity is disappointing,' snarled Big Wig, 'but predictable. Which is why I installed this.'

She pointed at the ceiling. There was a clear sheet of glass, and through that, Zac could see what looked like a telescope on a mechanical arm. It was mounted on the roof.

'What is it?' asked Leonie.

'It's called the Statue-Maker,' replied Big Wig. 'Did you notice our sculpture garden out the front?'

'You mean the trees and flowers that were like stone?' asked Zac.

'Yes,' nodded Big Wig. 'We've discovered that if you capture lightning correctly, you can concentrate the electrons to fuse molecules together. It's sort of like drying glue really quickly. I've been testing it on all our plants, but you will have the honour of being the first person we test it on.'

'What a cool gadget!' Leonie marvelled.

Zac glared at her. She was becoming more evil like Caz every second!

'Come on, Gadget Girl,' said Big Wig. 'We're leaving. Rock Star will stay locked in this tower. I can control the Statue-Maker from outside with my remote. When the storm hits, Zac will be turned into a statue!'

Rain began to patter on the windows. Lightning rumbled in the sky.

'There's that storm now,' smirked Big Wig, flicking a switch. The Statue-Maker began to buzz. 'Goodbye, Rock Star.'

Big Wig and Leonie marched towards the door.

'Bye, *Choir Boy*,' said Leonie. 'I'll say hi to Caz for you.'

Then she pulled the door shut behind them, and Zac heard a key turning in the lock.

CHAPTER... ...TEN

Once the door was shut, Zac swung into action. He'd left the skeleton key in the lock, so he knew he couldn't get out through the door. And the lightning strikes were getting closer. There wasn't a second to waste!

Zac raced to the window and tried opening it. Luckily, it was unlocked.

Zac looked outside. The ground was a long way down – definitely too far to jump. But Zac had an idea. He pulled out the lollybag from Agent Hammer's party and rifled through it.

It didn't take him long to find what he was looking for. A mini bungy cord! It was ultra-lightweight, but also ultra-strong.

Zac quickly hooked one end of the bungy cord onto the window frame. Outside, the clouds were growing darker.

OK, here goes, he thought, knotting the other end of the bungy cord to his belt buckle. He climbed out the window frame, took a big breath, and then jumped.

SPROING!

Zac fell through the air. Just before he hit the ground, the bungy tightened and tossed him back up. Zac bounced up and down a few times before finally coming to a stop. Dangling just a metre from the ground, Zac untied the bungy cord and dropped down. Then he dashed towards the front gate. He had to get out of there!

RUMMMMBLE!

The sky turned silver as a massive bolt of lightning hit the house. There was a creaking, groaning noise. Zac looked over his shoulder as he ran.

Whoah! he thought, almost tripping over his own feet. The lightning had split the house apart. The whole mansion was collapsing! Sparks flew everywhere, like fireworks.

Then Zac noticed two dusty figures running from the rubble. It was Commander Big Wig and Leonie. He was relieved they were OK, even though they worked for BIG. Zac didn't like to see people get hurt.

'What happened?' he heard Leonie whimper. Suddenly she didn't seem quite so brave.

'The controls on the Statue-Maker must have been up too high!' growled the Commander. 'It short-circuited the entire house and blew it up. That's two years of research ruined! But at least we've got rid of that pesky Zac Power.'

'Help!' Leonie squealed suddenly.

Zac laughed as he watched from behind the front gate. The Knight had survived the collapse, too. It was chasing Leonie around, waving its sword in the air.

'Show some guts, Agent Gadget Girl,' snapped Big Wig.

'I can't,' cried Leonie. 'I've swallowed my No-Fear Gum!'

Zac turned away from the house and caught sight of the Dragonfly Commuter-Scooter parked across the street.

Cool, he thought. *Looks like I've got my ride home!*

There was one final burst of sparks from the rubble of the haunted house, and then everything went quiet. The storm clouds were fading away.

Zac's SpyPad beeped to show it had finally picked up a signal. As Zac climbed onto the scooter, he called Leon to tell him he was on his way home.

'Glad to hear you're safe, Zac,' said

Leon. 'Nice work, too.'

Zac nodded. It was only 9:30am, so he still had heaps of time to relax before he went and saw the movie *Ghost Fighter* with his friends.

Awesome, thought Zac. He suddenly felt hungry. *And I want breakfast, too.*

'Oh, one more thing,' added Leon through the SpyPad. 'I haven't finished installing all those energy-saving light bulbs. You've got to help me before you go see your movie!'

Zac groaned. He really didn't feel like dealing with light bulbs right now. But a promise was a promise. He said goodbye to Leon and hung up.

Oh well, at least I can scare Leon with that fake huntsman spider I found, Zac grinned to himself as he revved the Dragonfly scooter. *Should make changing light bulbs a bit more interesting!*

For freebies, downloads
and info about other
Zac Power books, go to

www.zacpower.com